SPORTS CLINIC

TRACK AND FIELD:
Track Events

Luke Thompson

HIGH
interest
books

Children's Press
A Division of Scholastic Inc.
New York / Toronto / London / Auckland / Sydney
Mexico City / New Delhi / Hong Kong
Danbury, Connecticut

Thanks to David Bowden and the girls' and boys' track and field teams of Boyd Anderson High School, Ft. Lauderdale, FL

Book Design: Victoria Johnson
Contributing Editor: Eric Fein

Photo Credits: Cover and all photos by Maura Boruchow and Cindy Reiman except: p. 4 © Dimitri Lundt/Corbis; p. 39 © TempSport/Corbis

Visit Children's Press on the Internet at:
http://publishing.grolier.com

Library of Congress Cataloging-in-Publication Data

Thompson, Luke.
    Track and field : track events / Luke Thompson.
      p. cm. — (Sports clinic)
    Includes bibliographical references and index.
    ISBN 0-516-23168-5 (lib. bdg.) — ISBN 0-516-29564-0 (pbk.)
    1. Track-athletics—Juvenile literature. [1. Track and field.] I. Title. II. Series.

GV1060.55 .T56 2001
796.42—dc21

                                                                    00-066043

CONTENTS

INTRODUCTION

"I'll race you to the corner!" Almost everyone has heard that phrase. We've all run races when we were kids. Those races were not timed or run by trained runners. Organized track races, however, have rules that every runner needs to follow. Runners and trainers even use special language when they talk about track events.

Joining your track team at school gives you the chance to test your speed against the speed of other runners. You can also attend track camps and join in local competitions. Track is a place to meet new people and make some friends, too. You'll find out whether you're better at sprinting or long-distance races. You will also learn how to stay healthy and fit.

This book teaches you the basics of track races. Running is good exercise. Joining the track team just may help you become a champion.

Running track is a great way to have fun and stay healthy.

Outdoor tracks are made to help runners' shoes grip the surface.

ONE

TRACK BASICS AND TRAINING

The Track

Track races are run around flat, oval tracks. Outdoor track surfaces usually are made of a rubber and stone mixture. This mixture is poured onto the track and hardens. This surface was invented to help a runner's shoes grip the track. Because it also is much softer than asphalt or concrete, this surface causes fewer injuries to runners. Some outdoor tracks use crushed stone that is packed down. Indoor tracks have rubber surfaces glued onto concrete or carpets tacked onto wood.

Outdoor tracks measure 400 meters (about 1,250 yards). This distance is measured around the first lane (the one closest to the center of the track).

All races are measured in meters because most countries use the metric system of measurement. Outdoor tracks have eight lanes. Some indoor tracks also have eight lanes, but indoor tracks are always shorter than outdoor tracks. This book focuses on races that are run on outdoor tracks.

Lanes

Each lane on a track is 2 1/2 feet wide. Most races begin and end with runners racing in their own lanes. All sprinters and hurdlers race in their own lanes. Some long-distance races begin with runners in lanes. After the first lap is completed, runners can move to the inside of the track.

During some races, runners must stay in their own lanes.

Runners are assigned to their lanes through a draw (choosing numbers). If they cross into another lane during the race, they are disqualified.

More than one race is held for competitions that have many runners. Heat races determine the fastest runners. The fastest two or three runners from each heat go on to the next race. The final race is made up of the fastest runners from all the heats.

Track Shoes

Runners use different kinds of shoes for different races. Sprinters and hurdlers use spiked shoes to build speed quickly as they blast out of the blocks and sprint down the track. If you don't have spiked shoes, a good pair of sneakers will protect your feet and help you grip the track. Long-distance runners use shoes that grip the track and cushion the feet. These shoes also have wide soles and air pockets or soft rubber cushioning.

Starting Blocks

Sprint and hurdle runners use starting blocks to get a quick start. Starting blocks are metal plates fixed onto a metal bar at an angle. The bars have metal pins that fit into holes in the track in each lane at the starting line. They're called "blocks" because the metal plates block a runner's shoes from sliding backward on a fast start.

Starting blocks can be set in different positions. Some runners like the blocks close together

Runners use starting blocks to get off to a fast start.

so that their feet are close together when they start. Other runners prefer the blocks farther apart. Either way, the idea is to give runners blocks to push off from at the start of each race. Runners call this "exploding" out of the blocks.

Exploding out of the blocks from an inside lane on a good track is what every runner dreams of. However, no runner can get that chance without training hard.

Training Tip

Drink plenty of water before and after you train or run in a race. Experts agree that runners should drink at least eight glasses of water every day. Water feeds the muscles and protects them from cramping. Water also cleanses the body.

Getting your body ready to train is important for winning races. Warming up your muscles helps prevent injuries. Eating healthy foods and not smoking also are important to every runner's training.

Warming Up

Warm-ups loosen your muscles. Muscles work best when they are loose. In addition, loose muscles are less likely to be injured by running fast and hard. Runners have to stretch their legs before and after a practice or race. Each stretch works a different muscle or muscle group.

All runners must stretch before and after races.

Thigh stretches should be done slowly and carefully.

Thigh Stretch

To stretch your thigh muscles, kneel on the ground and sit back on your heels. Slowly lower yourself onto your elbows. You'll feel your thigh muscles stretch as you lower yourself. Count to eight and then lower yourself onto your shoulders. This is the farthest you can stretch your thigh muscles. Count to eight again and then raise your body to the sitting position. Repeat this stretch five times before going on to the next stretch.

Calf stretches help
avoid hamstring pulls.

The key to the thigh stretch (and all stretches) is to work slowly. Don't lower yourself farther than you can without feeling pain. You will be able to stretch farther each time you do this exercise. Rest between each stretch.

Calf Stretch

First, sit on the ground with your legs straight out. Bend forward and grab your toes. Pull your toes toward you. You will feel your calf muscles stretch as you pull on your toes. Count to eight before raising yourself up. This stretch also works the hamstring. The hamstring is a large tendon connected to the back of the knee. Most running injuries are hamstring "pulls." A pull occurs when too much pressure is put on the hamstring until it tears. Some hamstring injuries can last for months. The best way to avoid hamstring problems is to stretch your legs and keep your muscles loose.

Try to hold each stretch for 8 seconds.

Eating Right and Staying Healthy

A good way to keep your body healthy is to eat the right foods. Fast foods may taste good, but they are loaded with fat and are low in vitamins and minerals. Fatty diets also slow you down. Slow muscles are the enemies of all athletes. Runners need muscles that are ready to work for them.

Training Tip

Eating fruits and vegetables gives your body vitamins and minerals that you need to work better and fight disease. Apples, grapes, and oranges are loaded with Vitamin C. Vitamin C fights disease. Bananas have potassium, which helps muscles work longer without tiring and keeps them from cramping.

The Food Pyramid

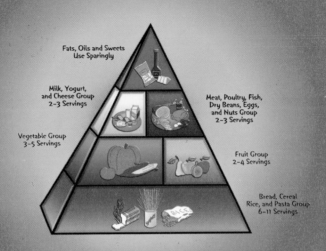

Fats, Oils and Sweets
Use Sparingly

Milk, Yogurt,
and Cheese Group
2-3 Servings

Meat, Poultry, Fish,
Dry Beans, Eggs,
and Nuts Group
2-3 Servings

Vegetable Group
3-5 Servings

Fruit Group
2-4 Servings

Bread, Cereal
Rice, and Pasta Group
6-11 Servings

A Guide to Daily Food Choices

The Food Pyramid

Dieticians study the quality of foods. They recommend eating a variety of foods from each of the four food groups. The food pyramid shows you which foods to eat so that you can stay healthy and strong. You should eat more foods from the bottom of the pyramid (breads and grains) than from the top (sugars and fats).

Sprint races are all about speed.

SPRINT RACES

The Dash Races

Sprint races are races that are less than 800 meters. Sprint races are all about speed. Sprinters explode out of the blocks and run as hard as they can to the finish line. Track competitions hold three sprint races: the 100-meter, 200-meter, and 400-meter dashes.

In the 100-meter dash, all runners start at the same line. This race is the shortest dash and is run down the straightaway to the finish line. The 200- and 400-meter races start runners at different points on the track. By starting at different points, each sprinter runs the same distance. This makes up for the longer distance that the sprinters in the outside lanes must run. When the racers get around the first curve, they draw even and race down the straightaway.

There are three parts to any sprint race: the start, the stretch, and the finish.

The Start

All sprints start from the starting block. You already know what the starting block is. Now you need to know how to use it. The purpose of the block is to allow a sprinter to spring forward at an efficient angle. The angle gives the runner time to build up speed much more quickly than starting a race in the standing position.

Figure 1

Figure 2

Figure 3

Most coaches agree that a sprinter should start out at a 45-degree angle to the ground (Figure 1). The hands should be on the ground with the fingers behind the starting line. The head and shoulders should be down and the hips up (Figure 2). One leg is forward in the block while the other leg is behind. This position lets the runner spring forward (explode) at the start and come up running (Figure 3). Exploding out of the blocks is a part of the sprint that all runners practice. They want to be comfortable coming out of the blocks to get the fastest start possible.

False Starts

Exploding out of the blocks is important to winning a race. Runners are often so anxious to explode out of the blocks that sometimes they jump before the gun sounds at the start of the race. A runner is allowed two false starts. A third false start disqualifies him or her from the race.

The Stretch

Sprinters come up from their start after 20 meters. Now they are running straight up and nearing top speed. They have entered the stretch part of the race. During the stretch, sprinters focus on their running stride.

A runner's stride is the way he or she transfers from one foot to the other. The stride is the distance between the front and back legs as each foot hits the ground. We

During the stretch, sprinters focus on how they are running.

all have a running stride. During a race, the goal is not to slow down or work too hard as you run toward the finish line. You want to keep your legs moving as quickly as possible without over-stretching them.

When your running stride is longer than your legs' natural stretch, you begin to leap off your back foot. Leaping to get a longer stride slows you down. To avoid leaping off your back foot, let each footfall roll from heel to toe during the stride. At the same time, allow your hips to move level with the ground and don't overstretch your legs.

Try to make your stride as smooth and relaxed as possible. Every runner's stride can be improved. As your stride gets better, so will your speed.

The Lean

Crossing the finish line is the final part of the race. Leaning forward as you cross the line can help you win a close race. The lean takes good timing. As you run up to the finish line, throw your arms back. When your arms go back, your chest shoots forward. This action pushes you an inch closer. Practice your lean every time you practice your sprint.

Runners have to throw their arms back to do a proper lean.

Sprinter's Drill

Jog slowly while lifting up your knees as much as possible with each step. Stop the high-knee lifts every 10 meters. Sprint for 10 meters and then switch back. Do four or five rounds, then rest.

When doing the sprinter's drill, it is important to lift your knees as high as you can.

In relay races, a baton is passed from one runner to another.

THREE

RELAY RACES

Relay racing is the only real team sport in track and field. Each relay uses four runners who run the same distance. The first runner passes a baton to the next. The fourth runner carries the baton across the finish line. There are two relay races run at the high school level: the 4 x 100-meter relay and 4 x 400-meter relay.

The 4x100 Meter and 4x400 Meter Relays

In the 4 x 100-meter relay, four team members each run a 100-meter sprint. Each 100 meters is one "leg" of the race. In the 4 x 400-meter relay, each runner runs 400 meters. The 4 x 400-meter relay is made up of four 400-meter legs. The purpose of the baton is to mark the end of one leg and the beginning of the next.

Passing the Baton

Passing the baton from one leg runner to the next occurs in the exchange zone. The exchange zone in a 4 x 100-meter relay race is 20 meters long. If the baton is not passed inside the zone, the team is disqualified. There is no exchange zone in the 4 x 400-meter race because the runners are not moving as quickly. The final leg runner must cross the finish line holding the baton.

The easiest way to pass the baton is called the "up-sweep/palm-down pass." As the passing runner moves into the exchange zone, he or she brings the baton up from the waist. The receiving runner already has started to run. The receiving runner holds out a hand behind his or

In a 4 x 100-meter relay race, the baton can only be passed in the exchange zone.

her back. The hand is held open and should look like an upside-down V. The passing runner puts the baton into the V slot of the receiver's hand. This passing technique allows the two runners to pass the baton while running at top speed.

Relay Drill:
Slow Baton Exchange

This drill exercises your legs while you practice smooth baton passes. Get a team of three or four runners and a baton. Spread out around the track. Jog slowly around the track, one at a time. Each time you reach another runner, pass the baton using the up-sweep/palm-down pass.

In hurdle races, runners must jump over ten hurdles to get to the finish line.

HURDLE RACES

There are three hurdle races: the 100-meter, 110-meter, and 400-meter races. Women race the 100-meter hurdles. Men race the 110-meter hurdles. Both men and women race the 400-meter hurdles.

Each race has ten hurdles that the runners must jump to finish the race. Hurdles in the 110-meter race are placed 9.14 meters (10 yards) apart. Hurdles in the 100-meter race are placed 8.5 meters (9.3 yards) apart. For the 400-meter competition, the hurdles are 45 meters (49 yards) apart.

Good hurdlers can jump over the hurdles without changing the pace of their sprint. Without an even stride and pace, runners can "stutter step" as they approach each hurdle. This costs time.

Jumping Hurdles

The proper way to jump hurdles is at full speed with an equal number of steps between each hurdle (Figure 1). As you approach a hurdle, lift your lead leg up and over the hurdle. Stretch the lead leg straight as you use your back leg to jump the hurdle (Figure 2). Tuck your back leg into your hip as you clear the hurdle (Figure 3). A low back leg will hit the hurdle. This can knock the hurdle down and upset your stride.

As you cross the hurdle, bring your lead leg down and plant your foot. Your back leg will move forward naturally to pick up the stride (Figure 4). Now sprint to the next hurdle. Don't expect to be a good hurdler in one day. Hurdling requires time and patience.

Figure 1

Figure 2

Hurdles Drill:
Two-Stride Hurdle Jumping

This drill teaches you to pace your stride and use both legs as the lead. Set up five to ten low hurdles along a straightaway. Space the hurdles so that there is just enough room for two strides between them. (It may take some time to figure out how far apart the hurdles should be.) Practice clearing the hurdles using both legs as the lead. When you get used to this hurdle distance, move the hurdles three strides apart. Work your way up to the regulation distance for your race.

Figure 3

Figure 4

Distance races require more endurance than speed.

FIVE

DISTANCE RUNNING, STEEPLECHASE, AND RACEWALKING

Any race longer than 400 meters is a distance race. The 800-meter and 1,500-meter races are medium-distance races because they are less than a mile long. Anything over a mile is a long-distance race. Long-distance races include the 5,000-meter, the 10,000-meter, and the marathon (26 miles, 385 yards).

Distance Running

Distance running requires more endurance than speed. Being able to run without getting tired puts you in a good position to win a long-distance race. Building your endurance means training your body to run long distances. You also

must train your mind to help you overcome tired-
ness. Mental and physical strength is the key to
becoming a good long-distance runner.

Relaxation is one of the most important things to
learn. Any good runner will agree that keeping a
calm state of mind is essential when distance running. It is the best way to channel the body's poten-
tial energy. The body rarely gives up before the
brain.

As you practice distance running, you may notice
that sometimes your mind strays. You stop thinking
about running and think of something else. Then, all
of a sudden, you snap back and focus on running
again. This is a sign of relaxation. It means that your
level of endurance is increasing. The only way to
learn to relax and increase your endurance is to get
out and run as much as possible.

Long-distance runners need to stay relaxed during a race.

The steeplechase is an unusual but exciting event. Steeplechase combines distance running with obstacles. There are two kinds of obstacles in a steeplechase competition. The first is a stationary hurdle (one that does not fall down like a sprint hurdle). The second obstacle is the water-jump barrier. This is a hurdle followed by a shallow pit of water. The steeplechase is usually a 3000-meter race. Steeplechases that are run by younger athletes are much shorter.

Training to run steeplechases combines distance running with hurdling. Pacing your body for the long run is the key to good steeplechase races. You also must be able to jump hurdles when you are tired. Jumping hurdles gets harder and harder as the race continues. If you get too tired to clear the hurdles with one leap, you can put a foot on top of the hurdle to help you over. This technique costs time with regular hurdles, but it is the best way to get over a water jump. The fastest way to get over a water jump is to plant one foot on top of the barrier and leap as far as possible over the water. The water pit is 3.66 meters (12 feet) long. Jumping the entire pool is tough. Plan on getting your feet wet during a steeplechase.

The steeplechase combines distance running with obstacles.

Racewalking events are 10 kilometers (6.21 miles) long or longer. Racewalkers are not allowed to run. During a racewalking competition, judges watch the racers to make sure they walk only. When an athlete begins to run, both feet leave the ground at the same time for a fraction of a second.

Racewalkers must have one foot touching the ground at all times.

Keeping one foot on the ground at all times is not as easy as you might think. In the heat of competition, the body sometimes does what the mind tries to tell it not to do. A good way to help keep one foot on the ground at all times is to make use of your arms. Your arms swing much less when you run than when you walk. Exaggerating your arm swing as you walk focuses your mind on walking and not on running. Try it and see for yourself. You might even want to imagine that you are racing with your arms.

Distance Drill:
Interval Training

Interval training alternates running with walking to help build endurance. Start out running one lap at a time. Run the first lap at medium speed. After one lap, walk for 30 seconds and then start the next lap. Run ten laps this way. As your endurance improves, change the distance and number of repetitions.

NEW WORDS

baton a small, lightweight stick that is passed from one runner to the next in a relay race

disqualify to take a runner out of a race when he or she makes three false starts or crosses into another lane during certain types of races

efficient angle a starting position that gives the runner time to build speed more quickly than a standing position

exchange zone a 20-meter space in a track lane in which the baton must be passed

lane a 2 1/2 foot-wide section of a track where runners must stay during most races

leg the stretch that is run by a single member of a relay team

NEW WORDS

runner's stride the way a runner transfers from one foot to the other; the distance between the front and back legs as each foot hits the ground

sprinter a runner who runs in dash races

starting block the piece of equipment that a sprinter puts his or her feet in for a fast start

straightaway the front part of the track where short dash races are run

up-sweep/palm-down pass a style of passing the baton in which it is passed upward into a downward, outstretched palm

water-jump barrier an obstacle in a steeplechase race in which a hurdle is followed by a shallow pool of water

FOR FURTHER READING

Jackson, Colin and Gwen Torrence.
The Young Track and Field Athlete.
New York City, NY: DK Publishing, Inc., 1996.

Pont, Sally. *Finding Their Stride: A Team of Young Runners Races to the Finish*.
Orlando, FL: Harcourt Brace, 1999.

Wright, Gary. *Track and Field: A Step-by-Step Guide*. Mahwah, NJ: Troll Communications L.L.C., 1990.

Organizations

Track-and-field camps are located all over the United States. Your school or local college might have one. The USA Track & Field national organization lists dozens of youth camps across the country. Contact them to locate a camp in your area.

USA Track & Field
1 RCA Dome, Suite 140
Indianapolis, IN 46225
www.usatf.org/youth

Web Sites

Track & Field News
www.trackandfieldnews.com
Learn about your favorite track stars at this site. Find race results and search the record books. There are also listings of U.S. high school All-American teams.

RESOURCES

American Track & Field

www.runningnetwork.com/atf

You can use this site to find running events in your area. Learn training and competition tips from the pros. Find out what's happening in the world of running.

United States Olympic Committee

www.usoc.org

Here you can learn about all the Olympic sports, including track and field. Search for profiles of your favorite athletes. This site also has a museum that provides information about Olympic history.

INDEX

INDEX

About the Author

Luke Thompson was born in Delaware. He holds a degree in English Literature from James Madison University. He currently lives in Vail, Colorado.